A Cat in the Stable

Troon Harrison • Illustrated by Benrei Huang

A CAT IN THE STABLE

Text copyright © 2001 Augsburg Fortress
Illustration copyright © 2001 Benrei Huang

ISBN 0-8066-4057-X

The paper used in this publication meets the minimum requirements of American National Standard for Information Sciences—Permanence of Paper for Printed Library Materials, ANSI Z329.48-1984. ♾ ™

Printed in Hong Kong   AF 9-4057

05   04   03   02   01   1   2   3   4   5   6   7   8   9   10

For my mother, who took me to the crèche
every Christmas and who fed my strays.
—T. H.

To Chi, for we still have good faith in miracles.
—B. H.

Muffin curled up on Sophie's quilt every night. When Sophie rubbed his chin, the old cat purred. His tongue was rough as sandpaper, and his whiskers were tough as fishing line. Sophie loved him.

Every night Muffin kept Sophie warm. Every morning he ran downstairs and meowed for breakfast. When Sophie walked to kindergarten, Muffin's green eyes watched from the porch. When Sophie came home, Muffin strolled to meet her, waving his tail.

Then one day Muffin wasn't there.
"Where's Muffin?" Sophie asked,
dragging her backpack into the
kitchen.

Mama pulled out a kitchen chair
and lifted Sophie onto her lap.
"Muffin was an old cat," she said
gently, "and he had a very happy life.
Muffin died today while you were in
school."

"Will he come back?" Sophie asked.

Mama held her close and stroked
Sophie's hair. "No, Sophie," she
said. "Muffin won't come back."

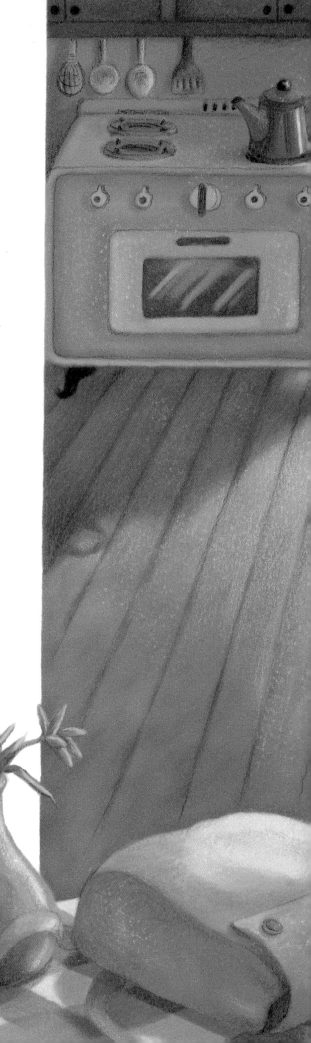

Later that afternoon, Papa dug a hole near the roses and buried Muffin's body. Mama and Sophie planted tulip bulbs on the grave. The bulbs were hard and dry.

"The tulips are dead," said Sophie.

"No," Mama said. "In the ground next spring they'll come to life and have beautiful flowers."

Sophie looked down at the grave. "Will Muffin come back to life in the ground?" she asked. Mama shook her head and hugged Sophie.

That night, after Mama tucked Sophie into bed, Sophie whispered under her quilt. "Dear God," she prayed, "make it spring soon, and bring Muffin back to life again. Amen."

When the first snow fell, Sophie felt happier. The world was bright and shining.

The church-school teacher said it was time to think about Christmas. "Everyone can make an animal for the nativity set," she said. Sophie liked the slippery feel of the clay. She shaped it into something round and brown.

"You can't have *that* in the nativity set," said the boy beside her.

"You're supposed to make sheep and camels," said a girl with ponytails.

"I can make a cat if I want!" said Sophie in her maddest voice.

"Ssshh," the teacher hushed. "Cats are God's creatures, too."

The week before Christmas, the nativity set was ready. It stood outside the church door. The clay animals looked warm lying in the hay. Sophie put her cat right beside the baby Jesus. Her teacher smiled, and Sophie smiled back.

"Jesus was born in a stable," the teacher said. "His birth was a Christmas miracle."

Sophie loved making cookies with Mama, using cutters shaped like bells and stars. Bits of sugary dough dissolved on her tongue. "Is Christmas the right time to get prayers answered?" Sophie asked.

"Only God knows the right time for everything," Mama answered.

"But Christmas is a good time for miracles," Sophie said. "My church-school teacher said so."

Mama looked at Sophie kindly. "Miracles don't happen often," she said. "You have to be ready for them."

At school, Sophie's class wrote letters. *Dear Santa*, everyone printed, *Here is what I want for Christmas . . .*

Dear God, Sophie printed, *I want a Christmas miracle. Please bring Muffin back.* On the bottom she stuck a shiny gold star from the sticker tray. The teacher had brought in a special red box for the letters. The other children dropped theirs through the slot, but Sophie hid her letter in her pocket.

Walking home after school, she stopped at church and slipped her letter to God underneath the hay in the nativity set.

On Christmas Eve, Sophie said her prayers and then lay in bed listening. Suddenly, she jumped out of bed and ran to the window. In the dark a cat had meowed! She pressed her nose to the cold glass. Empty snow sparkled in the starlight. Slowly, Sophie went back to bed.

On Christmas morning, Sophie's stocking bulged, but her bed was empty. No Muffin purred there. Sadly she stared at the rumpled quilt. It wasn't fair! God could bring tulips back to life. He could bring baby Jesus back every Christmas. Why couldn't he bring Muffin back to live at Sophie's house?

At church, Sophie was too sad to sing Christmas carols. She stared at her hymnbook, and tears began to run down her cheeks. Suddenly, Sophie couldn't sit still any longer. Her feet clattered as she ran past the singing people.

She grabbed her coat and rushed out into the bright wind. She would get her letter back from the nativity set. She would tear it to pieces. Stupid letter!

Sophie reached a hand into the hay. She couldn't see properly. The sun glittered in her tears.

Sophie gasped. Her fingers had touched something soft and warm. Her face was shining when Mama came up to her.

"What is it?" Mama asked softly.

The cat began to purr when Sophie stroked under its chin. Its tickling whiskers were tough as fishing line.

"It's that stray cat the neighbors have been talking about," Mama said, laughing. "It's found a warm place in the stable."

The cat was thin and orange. Its eyes were yellow, not green like Muffin's. But Sophie knew it was the answer God had sent her. Her heart grew big, making room for love.

"I'm going to call this cat Miracle," Sophie said. "It's going to sleep on my bed."

"Yes," Mama agreed. "God must have known this young cat needed a little girl."

Sophie lifted the cat out from among the nativity animals.

The church doors opened and people crunched into the snow. Papa hugged one arm around Sophie and one around Mama as the Christmas bells rang out.

Inside Sophie's coat, the cat purred
all the way home.